Mountain climbing?

says Sarah.

Quack!

says Duck,
shaking his head.

Figure skating?

says Sarah.

Quack!

Chair racing?

Quack!

Duck points at the book.

I've got an idea, Duck.

says Sarah.

Here you go -
put this on.

Duck makes a very handsome penguin.
Sarah makes a very smart . . .

. . . zookeeper!

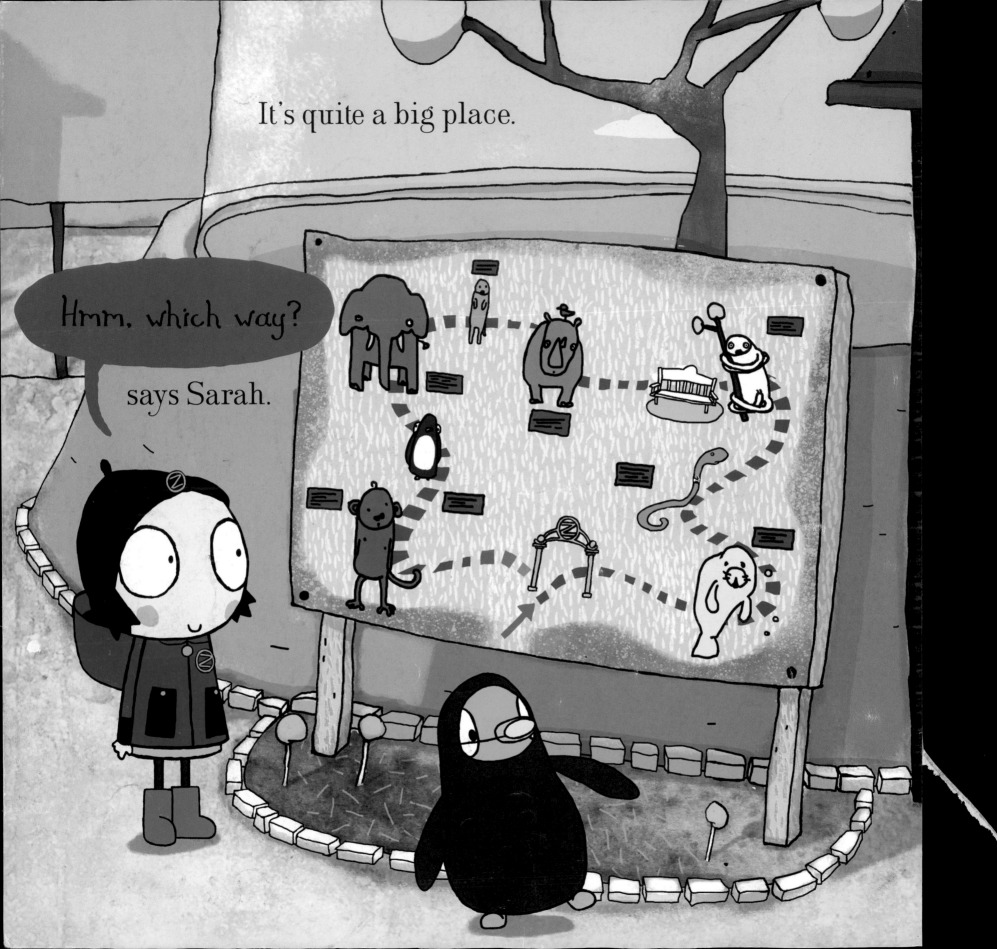

Oh, they have sea cows – like my poster. But that's not a penguin.

That's not a penguin.

Where is Duck going?

Oh look! Duck seems to have found the penguins.

THIS WAY!

It's not long before Duck looks quite at home.

First Duck tries
walking like a penguin . . .

waddle
waddle

Whoosh

then **sliding** like
a penguin . . .

then *oops!*
Slipping . . .

just like a **real** penguin.

But hello – who's this? It's the zookeeper
so it must be feeding time!

Come on now, chaps! There's work to be done.
You're the new zookeeper, aren't you?

Me? Umm, yes. OK!

says Sarah.

It's more difficult **feeding** penguins than it looks.

And it's more difficult **catching** fish than it looks too.

Oh dear, Duck.

Oh, now's your chance. Here comes **another** ...

Well done, Duck!

It looks like Duck has had **enough** of being a penguin.

Hold on tight, Sarah!

Oooooohhhh!
Thank you, Duck!

says Sarah.

It's been a **very** exciting day, hasn't it?
And look – this sea cow is just like
the one from Sarah's poster.

Would you like to be a sea cow, Sarah?

The End